LONDON LANDMARKS
from the Air

LONDON LANDMARKS
from the Air

PHOTOGRAPHS BY JASON HAWKES

EBURY PRESS
LONDON

First published in 1996 by Ebury Press

1 3 5 7 9 10 8 6 4 2

Photographs copyright © Jason Hawkes 1992, 1996
Text copyright © Ebury Press 1996
The photographs on pages 2, 36, 47, 56, 88 and 93 are reproduced by
permission of Aerofilms.

All the photographs in this book, and thousands more of London and Britain,
are available from Jason's library on 0171 486 2800

Ebury Press
Random House · 20 Vauxhall Bridge Road · London SW1V 2SA

Random House Australia (Pty) Limited
20 Alfred Street · Milsons Point · Sydney · New South Wales 2061 · Australia

Random House New Zealand Limited
18 Poland Road · Glenfield · Auckland 10 · New Zealand

Random House South Africa (Pty) Limited
PO Box 337 · Bergvlei · South Africa

Random House UK Limited Reg. No. 954009
A CIP catalogue record for this book is available from the British Library

ISBN 0 09 182034 0

Designed by Martin Lovelock & Co

Printed in Italy by New Interlitho

INTRODUCTION

Even those who have lived in London all their lives, but only seen it from ground level, are often astonished by what is revealed through the lens of a camera aimed from a helicopter a few hundred feet up. Behind the most imposing facades, unexpected and intimate details appear; the full grandeur of a noble ground plan can only be fully appreciated from above; and sometimes even an architectural trick or illusion is exposed – as in the photographs of St Paul's Cathedral reproduced on pages 46–7 of this book.

London is a vast and cosmopolitan city, with a population of over six million and covering an area of over 600 square miles. Each year over ten million overseas visitors come to London, making tourism the third largest industry in the city. But despite its size, it remains curiously intimate and accessible, an agglomeration of small towns and villages each with their high street and local shops and pubs. Unlike some of the European capital cities, there is little in the way of grand and monumental planning, no great tree-lined boulevards radiating from central axes as in Paris, no triumphal gates and arches as in Berlin or Rome. Central London retains many of its medieval and 18th-century street plans, and much of its 18th- and 19th-century architecture. And within it can be discovered an unparalleled range of historic sites and buildings – many of them best appreciated from above.

This book takes us on an aerial tour, starting from where most visitors begin: Parliament Square and Big Ben. There are four sections to this tour. First we explore the heart of London, from Westminster by the river to Hyde Park, and from Kensington in the west to King's Cross. Next we look north, from Regent's Park to Hampstead. Then we travel eastward down the river, from St Paul's Cathedral to the Tower of London, and onward past the new Docklands development to Greenwich and Blackheath. Finally we travel back along the southern bank of the river, looking south towards Crystal Palace and Wimbledon, and on past Chelsea, Kew and Richmond to the crowning glory of Henry VIII's great palace at Hampton Court. Every major London landmark is covered on the way, seen at different seasons of the year and in the varied light of different times of day.

London is blessed with finer parks than any other comparable city, and of course the aerial view gives us an exceptional appreciation of them. Because of the climate they remain green throughout the year, and they are beautifully kept and maintained. We have a bird's-eye view here of the private gardens of Buckingham Palace and of St James's Park; these almost link with Hyde Park, which merges westwards into Kensington Gardens; nearby to the north is Regent's Park, and not far beyond lies the great sweep of Hampstead Heath. To the west, we fly over Kew Gardens and the grounds of Syon House, take in the vast acreage of Richmond Park, and arrive at the magnificently landscaped gardens and park at Hampton Court. And in between these green acres we have taken a privileged airborne view of one of the most richly varied and historic cities in the world.

THE HOUSES OF PARLIAMENT

Both houses of the British parliament are housed in Sir
Charles Barry's and A.W. Pugin's gothic extravaganza on the
river at Westminster, the Lords in the foreground (near the
Victoria Tower) and the Commons at the eastern end.
Westminster Abbey, built in the true gothic style, can be
glimpsed beyond, and to its right the massive government
buildings that line Whitehall. The Post Office Tower can
be seen in the distance.

BIG BEN

The clock tower at the eastern end of the Houses of
Parliament, designed in the gothic style by Sir Charles
Barry in 1835 – after the medieval palace of Westminster
had been largely destroyed by a disastrous fire the year
before – is one of the most familiar of all sights in London.
Although the tower itself is now known as Big Ben, it is the
bell inside which was originally given the name – probably
after a famous boxer of the time, called Benjamin Caunt.

WESTMINSTER ABBEY

Consecrated in 1094, the present structure was begun in the reign of Henry III in 1245, and modelled on contemporary French examples such as the Sainte-Chapelle in Paris. It was designed as a royal church, for coronations and as a royal mausoleum, and is still used for the former purpose. Many national heroes are buried or memorialised here. In the foreground are the buildings of Westminster School.

WHITEHALL

The sombre government buildings of Whitehall are shown
on a cold winter's day. To the left is the Cenotaph, and
straight ahead is Downing Street where the Prime Minister's
office and residence is at number 10, with the Chancellor
of the Exchequer's next door. The walled garden of number
10 backs on to the Horse Guards Parade, where military
ceremonies like Trooping the Colour take place each year.

THE BANQUETING HOUSE

Dwarfed in this view by the massive and rather hideous
walls of the Ministry of Defence on the river front, the
historic Banqueting House in Whitehall (in the foreground)
is where Charles I was beheaded in January 1649. It
contains a magnificent ceiling painted by Rubens; and in
the 17th century elaborate masques were performed here.
Today it is often hired out for corporate entertainment.

WESTMINSTER CATHEDRAL

Here is the principal Roman Catholic church in Britain, built close to Victoria Station and completed in 1903 by J.F. Bentley to a design based on the cathedral in Sienna. The fine interior is, even today, incomplete: the east end is roofed in richly-coloured mosaics, but funds are still needed to complete this decoration of the whole building. Here on St Andrew's Day in 1995 the Queen became the first reigning sovereign for more than 400 years to attend a Roman Catholic service, ending the unhappy history that began in 1559 when Protestantism became the established church and the Catholics were driven underground.

12

The vista stretching from the palace down the Mall to Admiralty Arch (left) is one of the grandest in London, which unlike Paris has little in the way of such monumental planning. It was created early this century in Queen Victoria's memory, for she was the first monarch to live in the palace. In recent years Queen Elizabeth has allowed visitors into the palace [2]. In front is the Victoria Monument (below), the largest memorial to Britain's longest-reigning queen in London. It was designed by Sir Aston Webb, and the sculptor of the marble of the Queen herself was Sir Thomas Brock. The Queen's Gallery, adjoining the palace off Buckingham Palace Road (in the foreground of the picture on the next page), houses part of the incomparable royal art collection.

CARLTON GARDENS

Alongside the Mall, and overlooking St James's Park, is the
elegant terrace of Carlton Gardens designed in 1830 by
John Nash. It replaced the Prince Regent's palace there,
which he demolished a few years earlier; and this part of the
terrace replaced a famous garden created in the previous
century by his grandmother. Today it houses various
venerable societies and institutions.

17

ST JAMES'S PALACE

In the foreground St James's Palace presents a stern Tudor face to the park. Built in the 1530s by Henry VIII, it was lived in by the English monarchs for 300 years before Queen Victoria moved to Buckingham Palace. Here the Prince of Wales has his apartments, along with offices and flats for royal staff. Just beyond is Clarence House, the residence of Queen Elizabeth the Queen Mother; and to the right is the magnificent and recently restored Spencer House, looking out over Green Park.

HYDE PARK CORNER

Constitution Arch, in the centre of the traffic circle around Hyde Park Corner, was designed in 1825 by Decimus Burton and now stands directly in line with Constitution Hill leading up from the Mall. Just over the road is Apsley House, where the 1st Duke of Wellington once lived and which used to be known as No 1 London. The present Duke still keeps an apartment upstairs, but the remainder is a much-visited museum devoted to the victor of Waterloo and his achievements.

HYDE PARK

Kensington Gardens and Hyde Park, separated by the
Serpentine, stretch across the centre of London from
Mayfair to Kensington and provide Londoners with a
wonderful draught of fresh air and peace. Seen here from
the east, the Round Pond (built by Queen Caroline,
George II's wife, in 1728) can be seen glistening in the
distance. In the foreground is Marble Arch, and the
Bayswater Road leads westward towards Notting Hill.

THE HILTON HOTEL

This tower over-looking Hyde Park was one of the highest buildings in London when it was erected in the early 1960s, and the restaurant at the top still commands fine views over the park and southwards towards the gardens of Buckingham Palace.

KENSINGTON PALACE

On the western edge of
Kensington Gardens, the
palace was originally a more
modest building enlarged
by Sir Christopher Wren
for William III at the end
of the 17th century. Today
it houses five branches of
the royal family, including
the Princess of Wales and
her two sons. The state
apartments, seen here in the
foreground, have recently
been restored and are open
to the public. On the next
page, we see the whole of
Kensington Gardens from a
much greater altitude. To
the west of the Palace runs
Kensington Palace Gardens,
popularly known as
'Millionaire's Row', a
charming private street of
elegant mansions most of
which are now foreign
embassies.

VICTORIA & ALBERT MUSEUM

The long frontage of the Victoria & Albert Museum, designed by Francis Fowke, conceals immense galleries
devoted to the history of art and design, a treasure-house of jewellery, porcelain, sculpture, prints, fabrics, furniture
and much else. Beyond are the Natural History Museum and the Geological Museum, all part of the huge South
Kensington complex planned by Prince Albert in the mid-19th century as a centre for art and science. It includes
(though not in this view) the Science Museum, the Royal Albert Hall, the Royal College of Music, the Royal
College of Needlework and the Royal College of Organists; and the site covers 87 acres.

THE ROYAL ALBERT HALL

The circular dome of the Albert Hall is a familiar sight on the southern fringe of Hyde Park, and covers a hall capable of holding up to 8,000 for concerts and sporting events. The Henry Wood Promenade Concerts are held here each summer. The building was completed in 1871, and dedicated by Queen Victoria to the memory of her consort. Across the road, still hidden beneath protective covering while much-needed repairs are carried out, is the Albert Memorial – an extravagant edifice containing a huge seated statue of the Prince.

SLOANE SQUARE

At the eastern end of the fashionable King's Road in Chelsea, Sloane Square (left) contains an elegant department store, Peter Jones, and on the far side the Royal Court Theatre. Here George Bernard Shaw's plays were first performed at the end of the last century; and here too, under the directorship of George Devine, John Osborne's *Look Back in Anger* was presented in May 1956 – launching a new school of so-called 'kitchen-sink' drama.

CADOGAN PLACE

To the east of Sloane Street, Cadogan Place was laid out in the late
18th century when an advantageous marriage took place between
the 2nd Earl Cadogan and the daughter of Sir Hans Sloane.
Beneath the gardens is a large underground car park for shoppers
in nearby Knightsbridge, and in the foreground, down Pont Street,
are the elegant, gabled red-brick and terracotta houses built in the
style known as 'Pont Street Dutch'.

31

HARRODS

London's most famous department store first opened at the
Knightsbridge end of the Brompton Road in 1859. The
huge terracotta building, designed by Stevens and Munt
early this century, now covers nearly five acres on six floors
– and there is little that cannot be bought there. Among its
highlights are the richly-tiled food halls, where luxury
provisions of every conceivable kind are on sale.

OXFORD STREET

One of London's premier shopping areas, Oxford Street
(opposite) snakes eastward from Marble Arch to Holborn
and is thronged with buses and eager shoppers. Major retail
chains have their flagship stores here. Each Christmas the
street is spectacularly illuminated, attracting huge crowds.
On the corner with Edgware Road, in the foreground, the
Odeon houses the largest cinema screen in London.

OXFORD CIRCUS

For shoppers in the teeming stores of Oxford Street and Regent Street, Oxford Circus is the centre of London. Carnaby Street, where swinging London in the 1960s reached its apotheosis, is nearby, as are great department stores like Selfridges and John Lewis.

CENTRE POINT

At the meeting of Oxford Street and Charing Cross Road, this large building designed by Richard Seifert has over the years been the source of controversy. Its architectural merits were not much valued when it went up in the mid-1960s; but the main objection of Londoners was that for twenty years it remained unoccupied. No one knew why the reclusive property developer who owned it sought no return on his investment. Today it is not only occupied but has been 'listed' as a building of outstanding merit.

PICCADILLY

The whole stretch of Piccadilly lies below us, from Green Park on the right, to Piccadilly Circus. Along this famous thoroughfare are such renowned stores as Fortnum & Mason and Hatchards. Burlington House, home of the Royal Acadamy, is in the foreground. On the corner of the park is the Ritz Hotel, where visitors can take tea in the fancifully gilded Palm Court.

PICCADILLY CIRCUS

Still the hub of the West End (though at one time it was known as the 'hub of the British Empire'), Piccadilly Circus (above) has been through many changes since it was designed in the 19th century by John Nash as a grand crossing for his thoroughfare from Carlton House to Regent's Park. The statue of Eros is a popular meeting place, and now no longer isolated on an island in the middle.

TRAFALGAR SQUARE

The late afternoon sun throws the shadow of Nelson's column
directly towards the entrance-portico of the National Gallery
(opposite), one of the great art museums of the world
containing masterpieces from every school of European art.
These include Leonardo's 'Virgin on the Rocks', Van Eyck's 'The
Arnolfini Marriage', Vermeer's 'Lady Standing at a Virginals',
works by all the great Impressionists, and a fine collection of
paintings by British artists. In the view above, taken on a wintry
day, we see over the Gallery and directly down Whitehall.

39

COVENT GARDEN

Until 1974 Covent Garden (left) housed the city's main fruit and vegetable market, but when that was moved over the river to Vauxhall the market buildings were redeveloped to become a fascinating medley of specialty shops and cafés where street buskers perform. The Royal Opera House stands nearby in Bow Street, and at the western end we can see the four-columned portico of St Paul's church, designed in the early 17th century by Inigo Jones and known as the actors' church.

THE LAW COURTS

In the Strand, between the Aldwych and Fleet Street, are the Royal Courts of Justice, built in Victorian gothic style by G.E. Street. They are conveniently situated close to the Inns of Court, where barristers have their chambers.

TELECOM TOWER

This 620-foot tower, built in 1965, is now a familiar
landmark visible across London. The dishes on its sides
beam telecommunications to other towers many miles
away. Behind it we can see the massive white building
of the London University Senate House.

THE BRITISH MUSEUM

Housing one of the world's greatest collection of
antiquities, the British Museum first opened on this site in
1759. The present building, with its monumental neo-
classical frontage, was designed by Robert and Sydney
Smirke and completed in the 1840s.

THE TATE GALLERY

One of London's finest art museums, the Tate houses the nation's
premier collection of modern paintings and sculpture behind its
elegant portico fronting the Thames at Millbank (near Pimlico
tube station). In the Clore Gallery, an extension to the right of the
main building, is the huge collection of works by J.M.W. Turner
(1775-1851) which he bequeathed to the nation.

44

CHARING CROSS STATION

Railway stations are not generally objects of great beauty,
but the new 'post-modern' Charing Cross designed by Terry
Farrell in 1990 for one of the capital's key commuter
termini is already much admired by Londoners. Beyond it
can be seen Trafalgar Square and Nelson's Column, with the
National Gallery on the right.

45

ST PANCRAS STATION

Perhaps London's most dramatic railway station is
St Pancras, one of the main termini from the north. Its
romantic pinnacles, turrets and mansard roofs, recently
restored and cleaned, add dignity to a rather unprepossessing
neighbourhood. The new British Library can be seen under
construction next door. Beyond are acres of redundant train
yards and gas-holders; there are plans to redevelop this area
too, though some will miss its grubby charm.

MADAME TUSSAUD'S

This famous waxworks in the Marylebone Road
was founded in 1835 by Madame Tussaud, who
had been employed by Louis XVI to make wax figures
and fled to England during the French Revolution.
The exhibition is continually updated, and with its
Chamber of Horrors and Rock Circus is one of the
most popular tourist venues in London. Next door
is the London Planetarium.

REGENT'S PARK

When London embarked on its most rapid period of expansion in the 1820s, Regent's Park was planned with elegant terraces of housing around its edges to designs by John Nash. Here we can see the classical formality of Hanover and Sussex Terraces, with the boating lake in the foreground and the London Mosque just visible beyond. The park also includes the London Zoo at its northern end; and Queen Mary's Gardens to the south where the open-air theatre stages Shakespeare plays in the summer.

PARK CRESCENT

At the Southern end of Regent's Park, John Nash designed Park
Crescent, which was originally intended as a complete circus – but
the builder went bankrupt and it was never completed. Recently
restored, it still makes an elegant opening to the grand
thoroughfare that leads south to Piccadilly Circus.

THE LONDON MOSQUE

London's Asian population has expanded dramatically in recent
years, and in the late 1970s this exotic golden-domed building,
designed by Sir Frederick Gibberd, went up on the western edge of
Regent's Park. It works curiously well alongside the white 18th-
century Nash terraces close by.

51

LORD'S

London has many stadiums and sports grounds, but among the most famous is Lord's Cricket Ground in St John's Wood – the headquarters of world cricket since 1813 and the scene of nearly two centuries of Test Matches.

HAMPSTEAD

Until the 1830s Hampstead was still an isolated village on a hill to the north of the city, but much of its Georgian charm – and its status as a literary and artistic centre – survives. The vast and unkempt heath is a favourite playground for Londoners in search of fresh air and somewhere to fly their kites; and Kenwood House nearby, bequeathed to the nation by the Earl of Iveagh in 1927, contains a fine art collection. Open-air concerts are held there in the summer. In the picture opposite, Kenwood can just be seen in the distance.

SMITHFIELD

The largest meat, poultry and provisions market in
the world, Smithfield is set in an area of London
with a colourful history. For 700 years it was the
chief horse and cattle market of London; and until
the reign of Henry IV it was also the chief place of
execution. The main market building was built in
1867 by Sir Horace Jones.

THE BARBICAN CENTRE

In the 1960s the City fathers embarked on developing a
large site east of Aldersgate as a residential and arts centre,
and it opened in 1982. It contains three tall apartment
blocks, named Cromwell, Shakespeare and Lauderdale;
and a conglomeration of theatres, art galleries, concert halls
and cinemas. Both the Royal Shakespeare Company and
the London Symphony Orchestra are based here.

ST PAUL'S CATHEDRAL

Sir Christopher Wren's masterpiece, St Paul's was completed in 1709 to replace the medieval
cathedral destroyed – along with two-thirds of the rest of the city – in the Great Fire of
London in 1666. This aerial view (above) reveals what many do not realise – that the upper
and outer walls are false, and conceal buttresses supporting the inner walls of the nave. By
such artifice is the classical grandeur of the exterior achieved. This area of the city was
massively damaged by bombing in World War 2, but St Paul's miraculously escaped almost
unharmed – but now (opposite) most of the buildings surrounding it are modern.

THE BANK OF ENGLAND

In the heart of the City, the financial centre of London, seven streets converge (above). The Royal Exchange, the Bank of England and the Mansion House (the official residence of the Lord Mayor since 1752) and the Stock Exchange face one another at their confluence. The Bank itself is a vast edifice enclosing a garden with a fountain.

THE NATIONAL WESTMINSTER TOWER

This towering 42-storey black building in Bishopsgate (opposite) was designed in 1981 by Richard Seifert, the same architect who built the unpopular Centre Point (see page 35); but it has been much more admired. It is by far the tallest building in the City itself, though is now dwarfed by the Canary Wharf tower in Docklands.

LLOYD'S OF LONDON

The headquarters of London's insurance market was moved to this flamboyant modernist building, designed by Sir Richard Rogers, in the early 1980s, before this market entered a controversial period of scandal – and major losses for its wealthy private backers, the so-called 'Names' – in the 1990s. Sir Richard's hallmark as an architect is to display the workings of his buildings – heating pipes, electricity ducts etc – boldly on the exterior.

TOWER BRIDGE

Many visitors to London imagine that Tower Bridge is ancient, but despite its medieval appearance it was designed and built just over a century ago by Horace Jones. The towers and walkways now house a museum, and provide unparalleled views of the nearby Tower of London and up and down the river.

THE TOWER OF LONDON

One of Britain's premier tourist attractions, the Tower is some 900 years old, and has a dramatic and at times gory history. The central White Tower was built by William the Conqueror as a mark of his authority and to defend the city from invasion. The outer towers, walls and moat were added later. Here the Crown Jewels are housed.

St Katharine's dock

One of the first areas of London docklands to be redeveloped
in the 1980s, St Katharine's Dock is just east of Tower Bridge
and contains attractive residential and office premises and
a popular marina. Beyond is the Tower of London; and
HMS Belfast, a World War 2 cruiser which is now a floating
museum, is moored on the south bank of the river.

SOUTHWARK CATHEDRAL

Railway lines cut a massive swathe through south-east
London. Built in the 1830s, they catered for the huge population
expansion that came with the opening of the London docks.
Right in the foreground is the medieval Southwark Cathedral,
an architectural gem now set in unprepossessing surroundings.
But nearby are the recently excavated Rose Theatre and the
recently reconstructed Globe Theatre, with their Shakespearean
associations – and Shakespeare's younger brother Edmund is
buried in Southwark Cathedral churchyard.

CANARY WHARF

London's docklands, a vast area to the east of the City
which throughout the 19th century were a busy port at the
heart of a world-wide empire, have now been reclaimed as
a thriving commercial and residential centre. The Canary
Wharf development on the Isle of Dogs (opposite) includes
a vast tower which can be seen for miles in every direction.

THE QUEEN ELIZABETH II BRIDGE

Linking Dartford and Thurrock, way out towards the
Thames Estuary, this four-lane bridge (left) was opened in
1991 and is the largest cable-supported bridge in Europe.
The central span is high enough to allow ocean-going liners
to pass beneath. The most recent bridge to be built over the
Thames, it has helped greatly to reduce traffic congestion.

THE THAMES BARRIER

In the past there were frequent flood alerts in London
when the spring tides raised the river to dangerous levels.
The massive Thames Barrier was built in 1983 to control
this. Its ten steel-plated gates can be raised to wall off the
water and prevent flooding, but when retracted they allow
ships to pass up-river to the Canary Wharf docks.

GREENWICH

The Royal Naval College at Greenwich is one of the architectural gems of London, with buildings designed by the most brilliant architects of the 17th and 18th centuries – including Inigo Jones, Wren, Hawksmoor, Vanbrugh and James 'Athenian' Stuart. In 1995 the Royal Navy withdrew, however, and doubt remains about what future use these buildings may be put to. The National Maritime Museum nearby remains a highly popular attraction for visitors.

THE CUTTY SARK

This magnificent fully-rigged ship was built in 1869
as one of the last sailing ships to run the tea-route
to China, and is now in dry dock at Greenwich
where visitors can clamber aboard and imagine the
harsh conditions endured by its sailors on the
long voyage around the world.

BLACKHEATH

On the hill above the Greenwich Royal Observatory is the
broad open space of Blackheath (opposite), with its little
village of small shops and cafés adjoining. There are some
fine Georgian and early Victorian houses around its edge,
including an elegant crescent called the Paragon, and the
atmosphere is pleasantly rural.

THE NATIONAL THEATRE

This austere-looking grey concrete building on the South Bank houses the Royal National Theatre. Designed by Denys Lasdun, it opened in 1976 and has become London's leading theatrical venue, presenting a magnificent repertoire of classical and modern plays. There are three theatres inside, as well as pleasant bars, buffets and restaurants open throughout the day.

COUNTY HALL

Immediately across the river from the Houses of Parliament stands County Hall, which from 1922–86
housed the headquarters of London local government. After the Greater London Council was disbanded
in that year it remained empty while developers tried to decide what use to make of it. Currently
owned by a Japanese company, it is being transformed into two hotels, one luxury and one 'budget'.
Meanwhile, the Jubilee Way along its river frontage leads from Westminster Bridge downriver to the
Royal Festival Hall, London's premier concert hall, and to the rest of the South Bank arts complex.

LAMBETH PALACE

Across the river from Westminster is the London home of
the Archbishop of Canterbury. Built in the 15th century, it
was originally on the river's edge until an embankment was
created in the last century and a road driven through. The
church of St Mary, just to the right of the gatehouse in the
foreground, now houses the Museum of Garden History.

THE OVAL

London's second principal cricket ground after Lord's (see pages 52–3), and the headquarters of the Surrey Cricket Club, the Kennington Oval was originally intended at the beginning of the last century to be a circus of residential houses. But the development failed, and the ground was leased to the club by its owners, the Duchy of Cornwall. By tradition the last test match in any series is played here.

WIMBLEDON

The All England Tennis Club at Wimbledon, in
south-west London, is home each June to one of the
world's premier professional tennis championships.
The Centre Court (seen here with No 1 Court
alongside it) has seen many memorable matches
over the last century, and is hallowed ground for
tennis players of every nationality.

BATTERSEA
POWER STATION

Opened in 1937, and designed by Sir Giles Scott, this building (right)was hugely controversial at the time and widely disliked. Half a century later, when its use as a power station had become redundant and it was due to be demolished, opinion had changed and a preservation order was placed on it. But no developer has yet come forward to propose a viable new use for the building, and it lies gently decaying on the edge of the river near Battersea Park.

CRYSTAL PALACE

The television transmitter mast (opposite) at Sydenham in south London can be seen from as far away as Hampstead. The area is known as Crystal Palace because when the 1851 Great Exhibition in Hyde Park closed, Sir Joseph Paxton's huge glass and iron building was moved here to what was hoped would be a permanent site. But the building was destroyed by fire in the winter of 1936. Pleasure gardens remain.

THE RIVER AT CHELSEA

The Thames (opposite) runs eastward towards
the city (and eventually the sea) past leafy
Battersea Park and the 'peace pagoda' on the right,
and the gardens of Chelsea Hospital on the left –
where in May each year the world-famous Chelsea
Flower Show takes place beneath an enormous
marquee covering five acres.

CHELSEA HARBOUR

Built in the late 1980s, Chelsea Harbour is a luxurious office
and residential development surrounding a secluded marina
where luxury yachts and launches are berthed. It has brought
a welcome uplift to what had long been a seedy and run-
down area. The tower in the centre, The Belvedere, contains
a single apartment on each floor, making these twenty flats
among the most highly-priced in London.

THE ROYAL HOSPITAL, CHELSEA

In magnificent grounds just south of the King's Road stands Chelsea Hospital, built in 1682 by Charles II to the design of Sir Christopher Wren as a residential home for veteran soldiers. Today veterans still live there, exactly as they did three hundred years ago; and in their bright uniforms they are a familiar sight in the neighbourhood.

CHISWICK

Though close to the teeming traffic of the Great West
Road, Chiswick House in its little park remains a delightful
haven and a place of great architectural interest. Built by
the Earl of Burlington in 1729 in the Palladian style, it had
a huge influence on the design of houses for the nobility
throughout the country. The gardens, laid out by William
Kent, are also full of delights and surprising vistas.

SYON HOUSE

Syon has been the property of the Percy family, the
Dukes of Northumberland, since it was granted to them
by Elizabeth I in 1593. Its slightly austere walls conceal
magnificent state rooms decorated by Robert Adam, and
the park contains other delights for visitors – including a
butterfly house, and a commercial plant nursery. Across the
river are Kew Gardens, with the Palm House just visible.

KEW GARDENS

The botanical gardens at Kew are among the finest of their kind in the world, and date back to the mid-18th century when the current Prince and Princess of Wales (Prince Frederick and Princess Augusta) were hugely enthusiastic gardeners and the science of botany was in its infancy. The Palm House, seen here alongside its fine lake, was built a century later by Decimus Burton and is only one of several magnificent glass houses at Kew. The Pagoda (above), designed for Princess Augusta by Sir Williams Chambers, is another highlight. The gardens have something to show at every time of year, but highlights include the crocus carpet in early spring, and the rhododendrons in May.

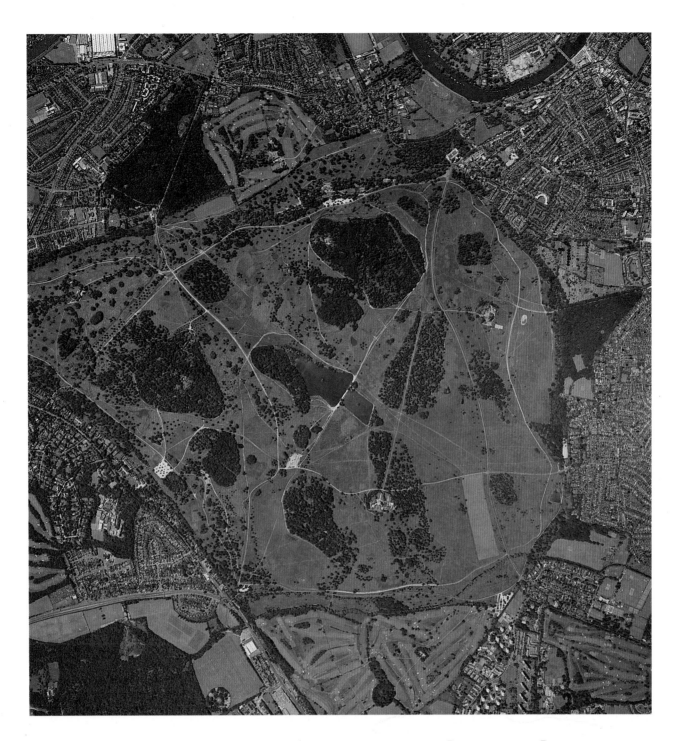

RICHMOND

This riverside town to the west of London is today
dominated by a large modern development on the
waterfront designed in a number of neo-classical styles
by Quinlan Terry. Criticised by purists, it is nonetheless
popular with the locals and attracts crowds in the summer
to its pubs and restaurants and to the bustle of the river –
as does Richmond Park nearby, with its magnificent old
tress and remarkably tame herds of deer.

RICHMOND PARK

Enclosed as a royal hunting ground by Charles I
in 1637, Richmond Park covers some 2,500 acres
and contains magnificent old oak trees, gardens and
plantations, and herds of red and fallow deer roaming
freely. There are several fine houses within the park,
including Thatched House Lodge, built in the
18th century by Sir Robert Walpole, and now the
home of Princess Alexandra.

HAMPTON COURT PALACE

Cardinal Wolsey built this magnificent palace for himself early in Henry VIII's reign, but as he fell from royal favour he presented it to the king. Henry enlarged it; and successive monarchs lived here and built on to it until the 18th century. No visitor to London should miss the experience of exploring the unique panorama of English history which it represents, or the magnificent gardens and park which surround it. Among the most popular highlights are the famous maze, and the beautifully restored Tudor kitchens.

INDEX